Fancy Fannie

Dave and Pat Sargent are longtime residents of Prairie Grove, Arkansas. Dave, a fourth-generation dairy farmer, began writing in early December 1990, and Pat, a former teacher, began writing shortly after. They enjoy the outdoors and have a real love for animals.

Fancy Fannie

By

Dave and Pat Sargent

Illustrated by
Jeane Huff

Ozark Publishing, Inc.
P.O. Box 228
Prairie Grove, AR 72753

Library of Congress cataloging-in-publication data

Sargent, Dave, 1941—
    Fancy Fannie / by Dave and Pat Sargent ; illus-
trated by Jeane Huff.
        p. cm.
    Summary: When Fancy Fannie wins the Grand
Champion trophy at the county's agricultural exhibi
tion, she begins to change her behavior and lose all her
heifer friends.
    ISBN 1-56763-372-2 (cb). — ISBN 1-56763-373-
0 (pb)
    [1. Cows—Fiction. 2. Agricultural
exhibitions—Fiction.   3. Fairs—Fiction.   4.
Behavior—Fiction.]
    I. Sargent, Pat, 1936—   .II. Huff, Jeane, 1946—
ill. III. Title.
    PZ7.S2465Fan   1998   97-27197
    [E]—dc21   CIP
                                                        AC

Printed in the United States of America

Inspired by

my love for Jersey cows, which I've milked most of my life.

Dedicated to

my beautiful granddaughter, Ashley.

Foreword

Fancy Fannie is a young heifer who is very beautiful, and she knows it. She likes to show off and because of this, loses all her friends.

Contents

Fancy Fannie

If you would like to have the authors of the Animal Pride Series visit your school, free of charge, call 1-800-321-5671 or 1-800-960-3876.

One

Training

It was the first of August, and the county fair was only two weeks away. April, Farmer John's middle daughter, had been working with her show heifer, getting her ready for the show. The county fair was the best show in the county. All the fancy heifers would do their very best to win first place at the show.

Farmer John gave each of his daughters a senior yearling to show. Each one picked out their own heifer. April was a good judge of fancy heifers. She looked them over, then picked Fancy Fannie. April worked with Fancy Fannie every day.

Early in the morning, April would get up and lead Fancy Fannie around the barnyard, teaching her how to walk and how to hold her head up.

After her morning training, April would lead Fancy Fannie to the pond where Fannie would get a drink of water. After she got a drink, Fancy Fannie was led back to her stall in the barn where she was given a good ration of grain and all the hay she could eat.

At noon Fancy Fannie was led, watered, and fed, and the process was repeated each and every night. This would be done every day until the county fair was over and the Grand Champion was presented the purple ribbon.

As the great day came closer, all the heifers got more nervous. That is, all but Fancy Fannie. Fancy Fannie thought she would win the show with ease. She thought she was the fanciest heifer in the whole world.

Fannie pranced around, holding her head up and making ugly faces at all the other heifers.

Finally, it was the day before the big show. Farmer John loaded all the heifers into his stock trailer and drove them to the county fair.

Each heifer got her own stall with lots of straw for a soft bed. All the heifers were so excited about the show that they could hardly sleep that night.

The next morning, the big day, April jumped up at five o'clock. She woke the heifers. They all had to be washed, groomed, walked, and fed before the show. April took extra special care with Fancy Fannie. She worked with her all morning making her look as beautiful as she could.

It was finally time for the big show. April led Fannie into the show ring. Fannie held her head high and strutted around the ring.

The judge watched Fancy for a long time before even looking at the other heifers. Then, after evaluating each entry, the judge motioned for the heifers to line up. Fancy Fannie won Best Heifer. Fancy received a blue ribbon.

Winning a blue ribbon meant Fancy Fannie would now compete for Best-of-Breed, and she would have to compete with all the Jerseys at the show, both calves and cows who had won first place in their class. This would be tough, for there were some real good-looking, fancy Jersey calves and cows at the show.

It was time. The judge called for all the first-place Jersey winners to come to the ring.

Fancy Fannie led the way with her head held high. All the cows, heifers, and calves who had won blue ribbons in their class were lined up in the ring. The judge knew from past experience that this would be no easy task. He looked at each entry. His eyes always came back to Fancy Fannie.

The judge walked around the ring and stopped beside Fancy.

In a loud, clear voice, the judge said, "The winner is Fancy Fannie!"

Two

Show Time

Now Fancy Fannie would have to compete with all the breeds for Best-of-Show overall. This meant she would have to compete with all the fancy Holsteins, Guernseys, Brown Swiss, and Aysheirs. This was going to be the toughest show yet.

It was time for the showdown. The fanciest cows in the county entered the show ring. Once again, with her head held high, Fancy Fannie led the way.

With April by her side, Fancy started around the ring. When all the fancy cows, heifers, and calves were lined up around the ring, the judge looked them over. He cleared his throat and announced, "This purple ribbon and Grand Champion trophy goes to the overall winner of all breeds."

April held her breath. The judge had stopped on the other side of the ring. After what seemed like an eternity, he started walking. He walked straight to Fancy and said to April, "Young lady, take your heifer to the center of the ring."

April's heart was pounding as she led Fancy to the center of the ring. She knew what this meant. And glancing at Fancy, April knew that Fancy understood, too.

The judge held up his hand. The crowd grew silent. "This purple ribbon and Grand Champion trophy goes to the overall Grand Champion winner, the fanciest heifer in the entire county, Fancy Fannie!"

The crowd cheered as April threw her arms around Fancy and kissed her on the side of her face.

The fair was over. The animals were loaded up and taken back to the farm. When they got home and out of the trailer, they all ran and jumped and bucked. They were all excited about being home again; that is, all but Fancy Fannie. When she got out of the trailer, she strutted around, holding her head up and being a show-off.

Every morning when the heifers woke up they would eat hay and play games. They loved to play hide-and-seek and catch-me-if-you-can. Fancy Fannie wouldn't play fair. All she wanted to do was strut around and show off. All the other heifers tried to ignore her, but she would run up in front of them and say, "Don't you wish you were as pretty as me?"

The more the heifers tried to ignore Fancy, the more she showed off. They got tired of Fancy Fannie being a show-off. They decided to slip away from Fancy while she was sleeping and go far away to another part of the pasture to play, a place where Fancy could not find them.

The next morning, bright and early, the heifers slipped off while Fancy was still asleep. When Fancy awoke, no one was around. She looked and looked and called and called, but no one answered.

Fancy thought, "Oh well, I'll just lie around here on the hill, and they will be back in a little while."

Fancy waited and waited. It

was getting on toward noon time, and still none of the heifers had come back. Fancy Fannie was lonesome. She didn't like to be by herself. All afternoon Fancy Fannie walked back and forth through the pasture hoping the other heifers would soon return.

The sun was going down, and there was still no sign of any of the other heifers. Then, just before dark, Fancy Fannie heard them coming out of the woods. She ran to meet them.

When Fancy reached the other heifers, she started strutting and showing off.

"Where have you guys been?" Fancy Fannie demanded. "I've looked everywhere for you. I've been lonesome!"

The heifers didn't answer. They just lay down and went to sleep. There was nothing for Fancy Fannie to do, so she went to sleep, too.

Early the next morning, when all the heifers woke up, they slipped off into the woods again, leaving Fancy Fannie asleep.

When Fancy woke up, she could not understand why everyone had run off and left her again. She became very sad. She decided to go and find the other heifers. She started off down through the woods. She searched and searched all morning long, but she couldn't find them.

Fancy Fannie got tired, so she went back to the top of the hill to take a nap. When she woke up, it was mid-afternoon. The other heifers were still gone. Fancy headed back into the woods, trying to find them.

Fancy hadn't traveled far when she got into a patch of cockleburs. They got in her tail and on her back, and she even had some in her ears. She looked terrible.

Three

No Friends

Fancy Fannie couldn't be seen by anyone looking like this. She lay down and started crying. "What am I going to do?" she thought.

Fancy ran to the pond and took a bath, but the cockleburs would not come out. She rubbed against a tree, but that did no good. The burs were going to ruin her looks forever.

Fancy Fannie went back to the top of the hill and cried and cried and cried. Her eyes were all red and swollen from crying so much.

Fancy Fannie thought that no one would have anything to do with her ever again, for now, she was the ugliest heifer in the herd.

As the sun went down and a blanket of darkness started covering the sky, the other heifers made their way out of the woods and back to the top of the hill. The top of the hill was their favorite place to sleep.

To Fancy Fannie's surprise, not a single heifer made fun of her. As a matter of fact, they didn't even seem to notice her. Well, that was fine with Fancy because she didn't want to be seen by anyone ever again.

When the heifers awoke the next morning and got ready to leave, they noticed that Fancy was nowhere around. They searched all over, but there was no Fancy to be found.

During the night Fancy Fannie had slipped off. She had decided to run away. She was never going to come back again. She went to the back side of the pasture and found a hole in the fence. She managed to squeeze through. She was now in the big cow pasture. There was nothing in this pasture but milk cows. Fancy Fannie looked around. All the milk cows were grazing.

The cows paid no attention to Fancy. Fancy saw Grandma Bell lying under a big oak tree, chewing her cud.

Fancy thought she would go over and talk to Grandma Bell. Grandma Bell was not Fancy's grandma. Everybody just called her Grandma Bell because she was the oldest cow in the herd. She was twenty-one years old now and was due to retire in February.

Fancy quietly lay down beside Grandma Bell without disturbing her. Grandma Bell was chewing her cud. She had both eyes closed, and her head was lying on the ground.

Fancy just lay there, watching Grandma Bell. She noticed that Grandma Bell had a few cockleburs in her tail and wondered how she

would get them out. She thought she
would wait until Grandma Bell was
through resting and then ask her.

Fancy Fannie waited at least thirty minutes, and Grandma Bell was still chewing her cud with her eyes closed.

Finally, Grandma Bell opened her eyes. She looked at Fancy and asked, "What are you doing over here with the milk cows, girl?"

"I ran away," Fancy Fannie replied.

"Farmer John is not going to like you being in this pasture with the milk cows," Grandma Bell said.

"I don't care," Fancy Fannie said. "I'm not ever going back to my pasture again. I have cockleburs all in my hair, and I don't want anyone to see me like this. Besides, no one wants to play with me anymore."

"Well, girl, you and I need to

have a long talk," Grandma Bell said. "First of all, cockleburs are a natural part of a cow's life. I get them in my hair every day, but that's nothing to fret about. They fall out after four or five days."

"I've heard talk," continued Grandma Bell. "It seems to me, girl, your biggest problem is what everyone thinks of you."

"What do you mean?" asked Fancy Fannie.

"You are a fancy heifer. That's why April named you Fancy Fannie. Now, being fancy is okay, but you are a show-off," Grandma Bell replied. "You think you are better than anyone else, and that's why no one wants to play with you. No one likes a show-off."

"Oh, you mean . . . so that's why they won't play with me? What can I do, Grandma Bell?" Fancy Fannie asked.

"Go back to your pasture and act the way you did before you won Grand Champion at the county show, and you will find that everyone will like you again. They'll start playing with you again if you stop being a show-off," Grandma Bell said.

Fancy Fannie crawled through the fence and went back to the top of the hill. She told all the heifers she was sorry for the way she had been acting.

Fancy Fannie was still a fancy heifer, but she never, ever again thought of herself as being better than anyone else.

Four

Jersey Facts

The Jersey is a small cow. They weigh from six hundred to eight hundred pounds. They are the most efficient of all milk cows. Jerseys can convert a higher feed-to-milk ratio than any other breed.

Jerseys are rugged animals. They can do well in rough country. In the United States, Jersey cows are raised mostly for their milk. Jersey bulls are used for breeding purposes.

Cattle are raised for their meat and milk, for their skins, and in some countries for their strength as draft animals. The process of domesticating cattle probably began during the Neolithic Period and was certainly well under way five to six thousand years ago.

Farmers, often in isolated areas, selected cattle that were best adapted to their particular environments and that yielded the products in greatest demand.

Robert Bakewell (1725-1795) of Dishley, England, is considered the founder of animal breeding and the person responsible for the development of many modern breeds. Bakewell's plan consisted of breeding the best to the best.

The Brahman breed was introduced from India. Cattle are not native to the Western Hemisphere; they were first brought to the West Indies in 1493 by Christopher Columbus. Then, Hernan Cortes took descendants of these cattle to Mexico, and they were eventually raised throughout the Southwest. They were a hardy, all-purpose cattle. Today's remnant population of pure Texas Longhorns are direct descendants of these early cattle.

In the early seventeenth century, English Shorthorn cattle were imported by colonists on the East Coast of the United States. These were dual- and triple-purpose cattle for producing meat, milk, and the tallow and hides that were important colonial export items. Settlers who moved westward took their cattle with them, especially the oxen that pulled the wagons and later supplied the power to break the tough prairie sod. By 1860 the cattle industry of the Corn Belt states was highly developed; that of the Great Plains and the mountain states was not fully stocked until the 1880s, however.